D1297028

The Tomtes' Christmas Porridge

Sven Nordqvist

In Scandinavian folklore, tomtes are little creatures who guard and help a family. Traditionally, a bowl of porridge is left out for the tomtes on Christmas night as a special gift to thank them for their protection.

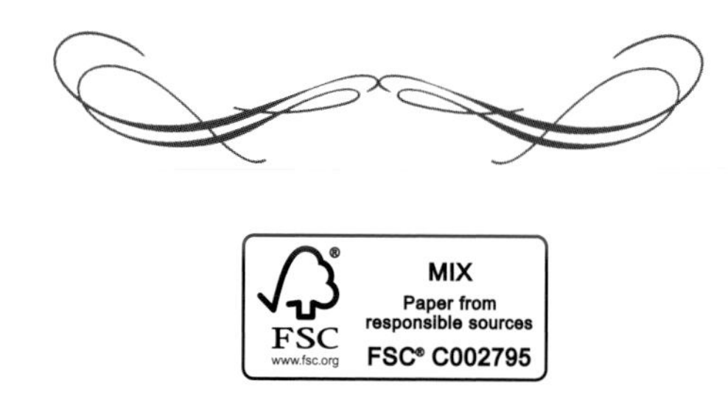

Translated by Polly Lawson

First published in Swedish as *Julgröten* by Bokförlaget Opal AB
This edition published by Floris Books in 2011
Fourth printing 2018

www.florisbooks.co.uk

British Library CIP data available
ISBN 978-086315-824-7
Printed in Latvia

It was Christmas Eve, and snow lay white and silent over the houses. Light shone brightly from the windows. Christmas dinner was nearly ready.

Papa tomte and his daughter Polka were in the hayloft, peeking through the holes the woodpeckers had made.

"Look, here comes the master," said Polka, "bringing all the family back from the station. Soon the children will give the animals in the barn their Christmas dinner."

"And then they will put out my Christmas porridge," said Papa tomte.

"You always go on and on about Christmas porridge," said Polka, "but Mama's porridge is just as good."

"That may be so," said Papa tomte, "but the porridge is a sign of respect, to say thank you for our help around the farm. I'll be angry if they don't say thank you. You see, my girl, when you have spent a whole year working and..."

"Yaaaaaaaaawww..." Polka let out a big yawn, and giggled.

"One day I will teach you some manners," Papa tomte sighed. "But that will have to wait because it's time for Christmas dinner."

"Yippee!" said Polka. "And then we'll see Father Christmas!"

"Yippee!" said Papa tomte. "And then we'll have our porridge."

The tomtes lived in the loft of the haybarn, behind a secret door that only they could see. Mama tomte was setting the table, and Polka's big brother Pulka was stirring the Christmas soup, made from herbs, berries and mushrooms that they had collected.

Tomte bread is made from four kinds of flour, and they drink special beer, which gets sweeter and weaker for younger tomtes, and stronger and richer for older tomtes. So little Pilka, who was four years old, could drink as much beer as Grandfather, who was 427.

SALT

Mama tomte was feeling worried. Like all mother tomtes she knew everything, even things that hadn't happened yet. So she might suddenly say to her husband, "Some burning coal just fell out of the fire. Quick! Put it out!"

Right now, Mama tomte knew that the family would forget to put out a bowl of Christmas porridge that evening. These days, people often forgot about the tomtes. They only cared about Father Christmas.

It had happened once before, a long time ago. Papa tomte had been so angry he had made the whole farm miserable for an entire year.

Mama tomte knew she had to do something.

"Is it time to collect the porridge?" Grandfather tomte asked.

"I don't want Christmas porridge," said little Pilka.

"It's too early," said Papa tomte. "Let's have our soup first."

But all he could think about was the Christmas porridge. "Well, I'll just have a look. You never know..."

When Papa tomte had gone, Mama tomte whispered to Polka and Pulka.

"You have to help me. The family are going to forget our porridge, and Papa will get angry. We have to remind them, but without being seen, or we could lose all our power."

She explained her plan and the children nodded.

Just then, Papa tomte came back. "No porridge yet," he said.

So they all sat down to Christmas dinner, and had soup, bread and beer, and told their favourite stories. Grandfather told a very long tale about something that had happened 150 years ago – but nobody minded.

Suddenly Mama tomte said, "Father Christmas is here! Let's go and see him."

"Yeeeessss!" shouted all three tomte children and ran off.

"Wait for us!" said Papa tomte.

The farm was full of secret doors and passageways that only the tomtes and mice knew were there. They could get into the house and on top of the big cupboard in the dining room without being seen.

The tomtes sat watching the family drinking coffee, eating dessert and talking. The children were waiting for Father Christmas.

The youngest girl, Anna, kept running up to her grandmother, asking, "When is he coming?"

Pilka was wondering the same thing. Then they heard someone stomping the snow off his feet outside, and knocking on the door.

"It's Father Christmas!" all the children shouted.

Through the door came a man with a long white beard and a sack on his back. He had a red coat and hat, just like the tomtes.

"Have you all been good?" Father Christmas asked the family in a deep voice.

"Any good tomte would know that without asking," grumbled Papa tomte.

Father Christmas sat down, opened his sack and handed out presents.

The tomtes watched, and tried to guess whether the children were pleased with their presents or not. This was one of their favourite games.

After Father Christmas had gone, the party continued. The tomtes enjoyed watching the excited people in the room. They loved it when the family were happy.

After a while, the mistress asked if anyone still had room for some Christmas porridge. Bowls were placed on the table and the cook brought out a big steaming pot of porridge.

This was the moment Mama tomte had been waiting for. Under no circumstances could Papa tomte see the people forgetting to put out the porridge for the tomtes!

"Papa, dear," said Mama tomte, "one of the sheep is trapped in the barn. Please go and set her free."

"But... they're about to serve my porridge!"

"Quick! She's in pain!" cried Mama tomte. "And mend the sheep pen while you're there. You should have done it years ago."

Papa tomte sighed and hurried off. Grandfather and Pilka had fallen asleep, which was just as well...

"Children," said Mama tomte, "it's time!"

Mama tomte and Pulka rushed downstairs and hid under a bench in the dining room. Polka ran into a secret passageway that led inside the grandfather clock.

Just as the master began to serve the porridge, Polka turned the cogs as hard as she could... and the clock struck eleven.

"What's that?" said the master. "It only struck ten a minute ago!" He looked at the grandfather clock and then at his watch. Everyone turned to see the big hand moving much too quickly around the clock face.

"What's the meaning of this?" said the master again. He walked slowly to the clock. The room was silent.

As the clock started to rattle and click and strike twelve, Mama tomte and Pulka scurried out from under the bench. Quick as mice, they climbed up onto the master's chair. As everyone stared at the clock, Mama tomte jumped onto the table and peeked over a porridge bowl.

She passed the porridge bowl down to Pulka and then jumped down onto the chair, and then onto the floor, where she took the bowl from Pulka. Then they picked up the bowl together and hurried away.

Nobody had seen them. The clock struck twelve.

"That is most extraordinary," the master said with an uncertain smile. He didn't know whether to laugh or be afraid. "Is this a joke or a ghost?"

He opened the clock and checked the pendulum.

The tomtes were almost out of the room when Mama tomte realised that there was no butter on the porridge! The butter was as important as the porridge itself. They had to go back.

"We won't make it!" Pulka whispered.

"Yes, we will. Quickly!"

Mama tomte climbed back up the chair and onto the table.

There was the butter dish. Thank goodness! Without looking round, she took a big scoop of butter and tossed it – *plop!* – into the porridge bowl.

Then she noticed that Anna was watching her. The little girl had seen everything. Not even a tiny tomte can throw a scoop of butter in front of a four year old without being seen. Their eyes met for a still, silent moment, then Mama tomte leaped off the table and ran out of the room.

Slowly Anna said, "Mama, there was a tomte here taking some butter."

Just then the clock stopped spinning and striking so everyone sat down to eat their Christmas porridge.

"Who's taken my porridge?" asked the master.

"It was the tomtes," said Anna. "I saw a mama tomte throw some butter into the porridge, and there was another tomte, and they ran away with the bowl. Out there!" She pointed to the hall.

The master nodded seriously, but behind his moustache he was smiling.

"You forgot to put out porridge for the tomtes," said Anna's grandmother. "You should be glad it was a mama tomte. If it had been a papa tomte, you would have been sorry."

The master left the table and opened the front door. Everybody followed.

In the snow on the steps was a round print and many tiny footprints leading off into the darkness towards the barn. They all stared as the little footprints were magically covered by snow. Then they went back inside.

They would never forget the tomtes' Christmas porridge again.

Papa tomte sat in his chair, feeling happy and full of porridge.

Grandfather tomte and the children were sleeping, and Mama tomte looked out of the window towards the house. She wondered if the family would remember to thank them next year. And she wondered if it mattered that Anna had seen her. It was probably all right for little children to see tomtes, she decided.

"What are you thinking about, my dear?" asked Papa tomte.

"Just what a good husband I have, who looks after everything the people can't do for themselves," she replied.

"Mmmm," said Papa tomte. "I wonder if I'll get as much butter on my porridge next year."